# THE
# BIGGEST
# BOY

BY KEVIN HENKES
ILLUSTRATED BY NANCY TAFURI

GREENWILLOW BOOKS • NEW YORK

For Laura
—K. H.

For Cristina
—N. T.

Watercolor inks and a black pen
were used for the full-color art.
The text type is Americana.

Text copyright © 1995
by Kevin Henkes
Illustrations copyright © 1995
by Nancy Tafuri

Printed and bound in Singapore by Tien Wah Press

The Library of Congress has cataloged
the Greenwillow Books edition of
The Biggest Boy as follows:

Henkes, Kevin.
The biggest boy / by Kevin Henkes;
pictures by Nancy Tafuri.
   p.   cm.
Summary: Billy and his parents
discuss how big he is getting.
ISBN 0-688-12829-7 (trade)
ISBN 0-688-12830-0 (lib. bdg.)
[1. Size—Fiction.]
I. Tafuri, Nancy, ill.   II. Title.
PZ7.H389Bi   1995   [E]—dc20
94-4574   CIP   AC

10 9 8 7 6 5 4 3 2

First Mulberry edition, 1998
ISBN 0-688-15841-2

This is Billy.

He is a big boy.
He can eat with a fork.
He can get dressed all alone.
And he can even reach some of
the cupboards in the kitchen.

Billy can put his boots on by himself (and snap them!).
He can answer the telephone.
And he can even help with the dishes.

"You are growing every day,"
  says his mother.
"Bigger and bigger and bigger,"
  says his father.
"Soon we'll have to buy you
  new pants," says his mother.
"And new shoes," says his father.
"I'll even be bigger than that,"
  says Billy.

"Soon you'll go to school,"
   says his mother.
"Soon you'll ride a bike,"
   says his father.
"Bigger," says Billy.
"How big?" says his mother.
"How big?" says his father.
"So big," says Billy, "I'll even
   be bigger than you. I'll be the
   biggest boy in the world."

"If you are the biggest boy," says his mother, "then you can wear the roof as a hat."

"You can stick your arms out the windows," says his father. "The house can be your jacket. Dogs and cats can live in your pockets." Billy giggles. "That's big!" he says.

"You won't have to fly to Grammy's," says his mother. "You can walk there in two steps."

"You will have to drink from the lakes," says his father. "And eat forty apples for a snack."

Billy giggles again. "Big!" he says.

"You can move the clouds by blowing on them," says his mother.

"You can hang a rainbow around your neck," says his father. Billy laughs and laughs.

"You will be so big," says his mother, "you can toss the sun up like a ball and catch it."

"And when the moon is thin
and curvy," says his father,
"you can wear it as a mustache."
Billy laughs and laughs and
laughs some more.

"But right now," says his mother, "you are just the right size for a big boy your age." "Just right," says his father.

"And right now it's bedtime
for a big boy your age,"
says his mother.
"Exactly," says his father.
Billy is such a big boy,
he climbs into bed by himself
and gets comfortable.

After one kiss and more kisses and saying good night,

Billy stares at the moon.
He holds his hand up to it,
and the moon is no bigger
than a marble.
"I really am the biggest boy,"
says Billy.

And in his dreams he <u>is</u>.